Homecoming

J18

For Emma and Rupert M.M.
For Oscar, Felix, Osian and Inigo P.B.

This is a work of fiction. Names, characters, places and incidents are
either the product of the author's imagination or, if real, are used
fictitiously. First published 2006 as "Singing for Mrs Pettigrew"
in *Singing for Mrs Pettigrew: A Story-maker's Journey* by
Walker Books Ltd, 87 Vauxhall Walk, London SE11 5HJ
This edition published 2012 as *Homecoming* • 10 9 8 7 6 5 4 3 2 1
Text © 2006 Michael Morpurgo • Illustrations © 2012 Peter Bailey
The right of Michael Morpurgo and Peter Bailey to be identified
as author and illustrator respectively of this work has been asserted
by them in accordance with the Copyright, Designs and Patents
Act 1988 • This book has been typeset in Bembo • Printed in China
All rights reserved. No part of this book may be reproduced,
transmitted or stored in an information retrieval system in any
form or by any means, graphic, electronic or mechanical, including
photocopying, taping and recording, without prior written
permission from the publisher. • British Library Cataloguing in
Publication Data: a catalogue record for this book is available from
the British Library • ISBN 978-1-4063-4107-2 • www.walker.co.uk

Homecoming

Michael Morpurgo

illustrated by
Peter Bailey

WALKER
BOOKS

I was near by anyway, so I had every excuse to do it, to ignore the old adage and do something I'd been thinking of doing for many years. "Never go back. Never go back." Those warning words kept repeating themselves in my head as I turned right at the crossroads outside Tillingham and began to walk the few miles along the road back to my childhood home in Bradwell, a place I'd last seen nearly fifty years before. I'd thought of it since, and often. I'd been there in my dreams, seen it so clearly in my mind, but of course I had always remembered it as it had been then.

Fifty years would have changed things a great deal, I knew that. But that was part of the reason for my going back that day, to discover how intact was the landscape of my memories.

I wondered if any of the people I had known then might still be there; the three Stebbing sisters perhaps, who lived together in the big house with honeysuckle over the porch, very proper people so Mother always wanted me to be on my best behaviour. It was no more than a stone's throw from the sea and there always seemed to be a gull perched on their chimney pot. I remembered how I'd fallen ignominiously into their goldfish pond and had to be dragged out and dried off by the stove in the kitchen with everyone looking askance at me, and my mother so ashamed. Would I meet Bennie, the village thug who had knocked me off my bike once because I stupidly wouldn't let him have one of my precious lemon sherbets? Would he still be living there? Would we recognize one another if we met?

The whole silly confrontation came back to me as I walked. If I'd had the wit to surrender just one lemon sherbet he probably wouldn't have pushed me, and I wouldn't have fallen into a bramble hedge and had to sit there humiliated and helpless as he collected up my entire bagful of scattered lemon sherbets, shook them triumphantly in my face, and then swaggered off with his cronies, all of them scoffing at me, and scoffing my sweets too. I touched my cheek then as I remembered the huge thorn I had found sticking into it, the point protruding inside my mouth. I could almost feel it again with my tongue, taste the blood. A lot would never have happened if I'd handed over a lemon sherbet that day.

That was when I thought of Mrs Pettigrew and her railway carriage and her dogs and her donkey, and the whole extraordinary story came flooding back crisp and clear, every detail of it, from the moment she found me sitting in the ditch holding my bleeding face and crying my heart out.

She helped me up onto my feet. She would take me to her home. "It isn't far," she said. "I call it Dusit. It is a Thai word which means 'halfway to heaven'." She had been a nurse in Thailand, she said, a long time ago when she was younger. She'd soon have that nasty thorn out. She'd soon stop it hurting. And she did.

The more I walked the more vivid it all became: the people, the faces, the whole life of the place where I'd grown up. Everyone in Bradwell seemed to me to have had a very particular character and reputation, unsurprising in a small village, I suppose: Colonel Burton with his clipped white moustache, who had a wife called Valerie, if I remembered right, with black pencilled eyebrows that gave her the look of someone permanently outraged – which she usually was. Neither the colonel nor his wife was to be argued with. They ruled the roost. They would shout at you if you dropped sweet papers in the village street or rode your bike on the pavement.

Mrs Parsons, whose voice chimed like the bell in her shop when you opened the door, liked to talk a lot. She was a gossip, Mother said, but she was always very kind. She would often drop an extra lemon sherbet into your paper bag after she had poured your quarter pound from the big glass jar on the counter. I had once thought of stealing that jar, of snatching it and running off out of the shop, making my getaway like a bank robber in the films. But I knew the police would come after me in their shiny black cars with their bells ringing, and then I'd have to go to prison and Mother would be cross. So I never did steal Mrs Parsons' lemon sherbet jar.

Then there was Mad Jack, as we called him, who clipped hedges and dug ditches and swept the village street. We'd often see him sitting on the churchyard wall by the mounting block eating his lunch. He'd be humming and swinging his legs. Mother said he'd been fine before he went off to the war, but he'd come back with some shrapnel from a shell in his head and never been right since, and we shouldn't call him Mad Jack, but we did. I'm ashamed to say we baited him sometimes too, perching alongside him on the wall, mimicking his humming and swinging our legs in time with his.

But Mrs Pettigrew remained a mystery to everyone. This was partly because she lived some distance from the village and was inclined to keep herself to herself. She only came into the village to go to church on Sundays, and then she'd sit at the back, always on her own. I used to sing in the church choir, mostly because Mother made me, but I did like dressing up in the black cassock and white surplice and we did have a choir outing once a year to the cinema in Southminster – that's where I first saw *Snow White* and *Bambi* and *Reach for the Sky.* I liked swinging the incense too, and sometimes I got to carry the cross, which made me feel very holy and very important.

I'd caught Mrs Pettigrew's eye once or twice as we processed by, but I'd always looked away. I'd never spoken to her. She smiled at people, but she rarely spoke to anyone; so no one spoke to her – not that I ever saw anyway. But there were reasons for this.

Mrs Pettigrew was different. For a start she didn't live in a house at all. She lived in a railway carriage, down by the sea wall with the great wide marsh all around her. Everyone called it Mrs Pettigrew's Marsh. I could see it best when I rode my bicycle along the sea wall. The railway carriage was painted brown and cream and the word PULLMAN was printed in big letters all along both sides above the windows. There were wooden steps up to the front door at one end, and a chimney at the other. The carriage was surrounded by trees and gardens, so I could only catch occasional glimpses of her and her dogs and her donkey, bees and hens. Tiny under her wide hat, she could often be seen planting out in her vegetable garden, or digging the dyke that ran around the garden like a moat, collecting honey from her beehives perhaps or feeding her hens. She was always outside somewhere, always busy. She walked or stood or sat very upright, I noticed, very neatly, and there was a serenity about her that made her unlike anyone else, and ageless too.

But she was different in another way. Mrs Pettigrew was not like the rest of us to look at, because Mrs Pettigrew was "foreign", from somewhere near China, I had been told. She did not dress like anyone else either. Apart from the wide-brimmed hat, she always wore a long black dress buttoned to the neck. And everything about her, her face and her hands, her feet, everything was tidy and tiny and trim, even her voice. She spoke softly to me as she helped me to my feet

that day, every word precisely articulated. She had no noticeable accent at all, but spoke English far too well, too meticulously, to have come from England.

So we walked side by side, her arm round me, a soothing silence between us, until we turned off the road onto the track that led across the marsh towards the sea wall in the distance. I could see smoke rising straight into the sky from the chimney of the railway carriage.

"There we are: Dusit," she said. "And look who is coming out to greet us."

Three greyhounds were bounding towards us followed by a donkey trotting purposefully but slowly behind them, wheezing at us rather than braying. Then they were gambolling all about us, and nudging us for attention. They were big and bustling, but I wasn't afraid because they had nothing in their eyes but welcome.

"I call the dogs Fast, Faster and Fastest," she told me.

"But the donkey doesn't like names. She thinks names are for silly creatures like people and dogs who can't recognize one another without them. So I call her simply Donkey." Mrs Pettigrew lowered her voice to a whisper. "She can't bray properly – tries all the time but she can't. She's very sensitive too; takes offence very easily." Mrs Pettigrew took me up the steps into her railway carriage home. "Sit down there by the window, in the light, so I can make your face better."

I was so distracted and absorbed by all I saw about me that I felt no pain as she cleaned my face, not even when she pulled out the thorn. She held it out to show me. It was truly a monster of a thorn. "The biggest and nastiest I have ever seen," she said, smiling at me. Without her hat on she was scarcely taller than I was. She made me wash out my mouth and bathed the hole in my cheek with antiseptic. Then she gave me some tea which tasted very strange but warmed me to the roots of my hair. "Jasmine tea,"

she said. "It is very healing, I find, very comforting. My sister sends it to me from Thailand."

The carriage was as neat and tidy as she was: a simple sitting room at the far end with just a couple of wicker chairs and a small table by the stove. And behind a half-drawn curtain I glimpsed a bed very low on the ground. There was no clutter, no pictures, no hangings, only a shelf of books that ran all the way round the carriage from end to end. From where I was sitting I could see out over the garden, then through the trees to the open marsh beyond.

"Do you like my house, Michael?" She did not give me time to reply. "I read many books, as you see," she said. I was wondering how it was that she knew my name, when she told me. "I see you in the village sometimes, don't I? You're in the choir, aren't you?" She leant forward. "And I expect you're wondering why Mrs Pettigrew lives in a railway carriage."

"Yes," I said.

The dogs had come in by now and were settling down at our feet, their eyes never leaving her, not for a moment, as if they were waiting for an old story they knew and loved.

"Then I'll tell you, shall I?" she began. "It was because we met on a train, Arthur and I – not this one, you understand, but one very much like it. We were in Thailand. I was returning from my grandmother's house to the city where I lived. Arthur was a botanist. He was travelling through Thailand collecting plants and studying them. He painted them and wrote books about them. He wrote three books; I have them all up there on my shelf. I will show you one day – would you like that? I never knew about plants until I met him, nor insects, nor all the wild creatures and birds around us, nor the stars in the sky. Arthur showed me all these things. He opened my eyes. For me it was all so exciting and new. He had such a knowledge of this wonderful world we live in, such a love for it too. He gave me that, and he gave me much more: he gave me his love too.

"Soon after we were married he brought me here to England on a great ship – this ship had three big funnels and a dance band – and he made me so happy. He said to me one day on board that ship, 'Mrs Pettigrew' – he always liked to call me this – 'Mrs Pettigrew, I want to live with you down on the marsh where I grew up as a boy.' The marsh was part of his father's farm, you see. 'It is a wild and wonderful place,' he told me, 'where on calm days you can hear the sea breathing gently beyond the sea wall, or on stormy days roaring like a dragon, where larks rise and sing on warm summer afternoons, where stars cascade on August nights.'

"'But where shall we live?' I asked him.

"'I have already thought of that, Mrs Pettigrew,' he said. 'Because we first met on a train, I shall buy a fine railway carriage for us to live in, a carriage fit for a princess. And all around it we shall make a perfect paradise and we shall live as we were meant to live, amongst our fellow creatures, as close to them as we can be. And we shall be happy there.'

"So we were, Michael. So we were. But only for seventeen short months, until one day there was an accident. We had a generator to make our electricity; Arthur was repairing it when the accident happened. He was very young. That was nearly twenty years ago now. I have been here ever since and I shall always be here. It is just as Arthur told me: a perfect paradise."

Donkey came in just then, clomping up the steps into the railway carriage, her ears going this way and that.

She must have felt she was being ignored or ostracized, probably both. Mrs Pettigrew shooed her out, but not before there was a terrific kerfuffle of wheezing and growling, of tumbling chairs and crashing crockery.

When I got home I told Mother everything that had happened. She took me to the doctor at once for a tetanus injection, which hurt much more than the thorn had, then put me to bed and went out – to sort out Bennie, she said. I told her not to, told her it would only make things worse. But she wouldn't listen. When she came back she brought me a bag of lemon sherbets. Bennie, she told me, had been marched down to Mrs Parsons' shop by his father and my mother, and they had made him buy me a bag of lemon sherbets with his own pocket money to replace the ones he'd pinched off me.

Mother had also cycled out to see Mrs Pettigrew to thank her. From that day on the two of them became the best of friends, which was wonderful for me because I was allowed to go cycling out to see Mrs Pettigrew as often as I liked. Sometimes Mother came with me, but mostly I went alone. I preferred it on my own.

I rode Donkey all over the marsh. She needed
no halter, no reins. She went where she wanted and
I went with her, followed always by Fast, Faster and
Fastest, who would chase rabbits and hares wherever

they found them. I was always muddled as to which dog was which, because they all ran unbelievably fast – standing start to full throttle in a few seconds. They rarely caught anything but they loved the chase.

With Mrs Pettigrew I learnt how to puff the bees to sleep before taking out the honeycomb. I collected eggs warm from the hens, dug up potatoes, pulled carrots, bottled plums and damsons in Kilner jars. (Ever since, whenever I see the blush on a plum I always think of Mrs Pettigrew.) And always Mrs Pettigrew would send me home afterwards with a present for Mother and me, a pot of honey perhaps or some sweetcorn from her garden.

Sometimes Mrs Pettigrew would take me along the sea wall all the way to St Peter's Chapel and back, the oldest chapel in England, she said. Once we stopped to watch a lark rising and rising, singing and singing so high in the blue we could see it no more. But the singing went on, and she said, "I remember a time – we were standing almost on this very same spot – when Arthur and I heard a lark singing just like that. I have never forgotten his words. 'I think it's singing for you,' he said, 'singing for Mrs Pettigrew.'"

Then there was the night in August when Mother and Mrs Pettigrew and I lay out on the grass in the garden gazing up at the shooting stars cascading across the sky above us, just as she had with Arthur, she said. How I wondered at the glory of it, and the sheer immensity of the universe. I was so glad then that Bennie had pushed me off my bike that day, so glad I had met Mrs Pettigrew, so glad I was alive. But soon after came the rumours and the meetings and the anger, and all the gladness was suddenly gone.

I don't remember how I heard about it first. It could have been in the playground at school, or Mother might have told me or even Mrs Pettigrew. It could have been Mrs Parsons in the shop. It doesn't matter. One way or another, everyone in the village and for miles around got to hear about it. Soon it was all anyone talked about. I didn't really understand

what it meant to start with. It was that first meeting in the village hall that brought it home to me. There were pictures and plans of a giant building pinned up on the wall for everyone to see. There was a model of it too, with the marsh all around and the sea wall running along behind it, and the blue sea beyond with models of fishing boats and yachts sailing by. That, I think, was when I truly began to comprehend the implication of what was going on, of what was actually being proposed. The men in suits sitting behind the table on the platform that evening made it quite clear.

They wanted to build a power station, but not just an ordinary power station, a huge newfangled atomic power station, the most modern design in the whole world, they said. They had decided to build it out on the marsh — and everyone knew by now they meant Mrs Pettigrew's Marsh. It was the best place, they said.

It was the safest place, they said, far enough outside the village and far enough away from London. I didn't understand then who the men in suits were, of course, but I did understand what they were telling us: that this atomic power station was necessary because it would provide cheaper electricity for all of us; that London, which was only fifty or so miles away, was growing fast and needed more electricity. Bradwell had been chosen because it was the perfect site, near the sea so the water could be used for cooling, and near to London, but not too near.

"If it's for Londoners, and if it's so safe, what's wrong with it being right in London then?" the colonel asked.

"They've got water there too, haven't they?" said Miss Blackwell, my teacher.

Mrs Parsons stood up then, beside herself with fury.

"Well, I think they want to build it out here miles away from London because it might blow up like that bomb in Hiroshima. That's what I think. I think it's wicked, wicked. And anyway, what about Mrs Pettigrew? She lives out there on the marsh. Where's she going to live?"

Beside me Mother was holding Mrs Pettigrew's hand and patting it as the argument raged on. There'd be any number of new jobs, said one side. There are plenty of jobs anyway, said the other side. It would be a great concrete monstrosity; it would blight the whole landscape. It would be well screened by trees, well landscaped; you'd hardly notice it; and anyway you'd get used to it soon enough once it was there. It would be clean too, no chimneys, no smoke. But what if there was an accident, if the radiation leaked out? What then?

Suddenly Mrs Pettigrew was on her feet. Maybe it was because she didn't speak for a while that everyone fell silent around her. When she did speak at last, her voice trembled. It trembled because she was trembling, her knuckles bone-white as she clutched Mother's hand. I can still remember what she said, almost word for word.

"Since I first heard about this I have read many

books. From these books I have learnt many important things. At the heart of an atomic power station there is a radioactive core. The energy this makes produces electricity. But this energy has to be used and controlled with very great care. Any mistake or any accident could cause this radioactive core to become unstable. This could lead to an explosion, which would be catastrophic, or there could be a leak of radiation into the atmosphere. Either of these would cause the greatest destruction to all forms of life, human beings, animals, birds, sea life and plants, for miles and miles around. But I am sure those who wish to build this power station have thought of all this and will make it as safe as possible. I am sure those who will operate it will be careful. But Arthur, my late husband, was careful too. He installed a simple generator for our home. He thought it was safe, but it killed him.

"So I ask you, gentlemen, to think again. Machines are not perfect. Science is not perfect. Mistakes can easily be made. Accidents can happen. I am sure you understand this. And there is something else I would like you to understand. For me the place where you would build your atomic power station is home. You may have decided it is an uninteresting place and unimportant, just home to one strange lady who lives there on the marsh with her donkey and her dogs and her hens. But it is not uninteresting and it is not unimportant. It is not just my home either, but home also for curlews and gulls and wild geese and teal and redshanks and barn owls and kestrels. There are herons, and larks. The otter lives here and the fox comes to visit, the badger too, even sometimes the deer. And amongst the marsh grass and reeds and the bulrushes live a thousand different insects, and a thousand different plants.

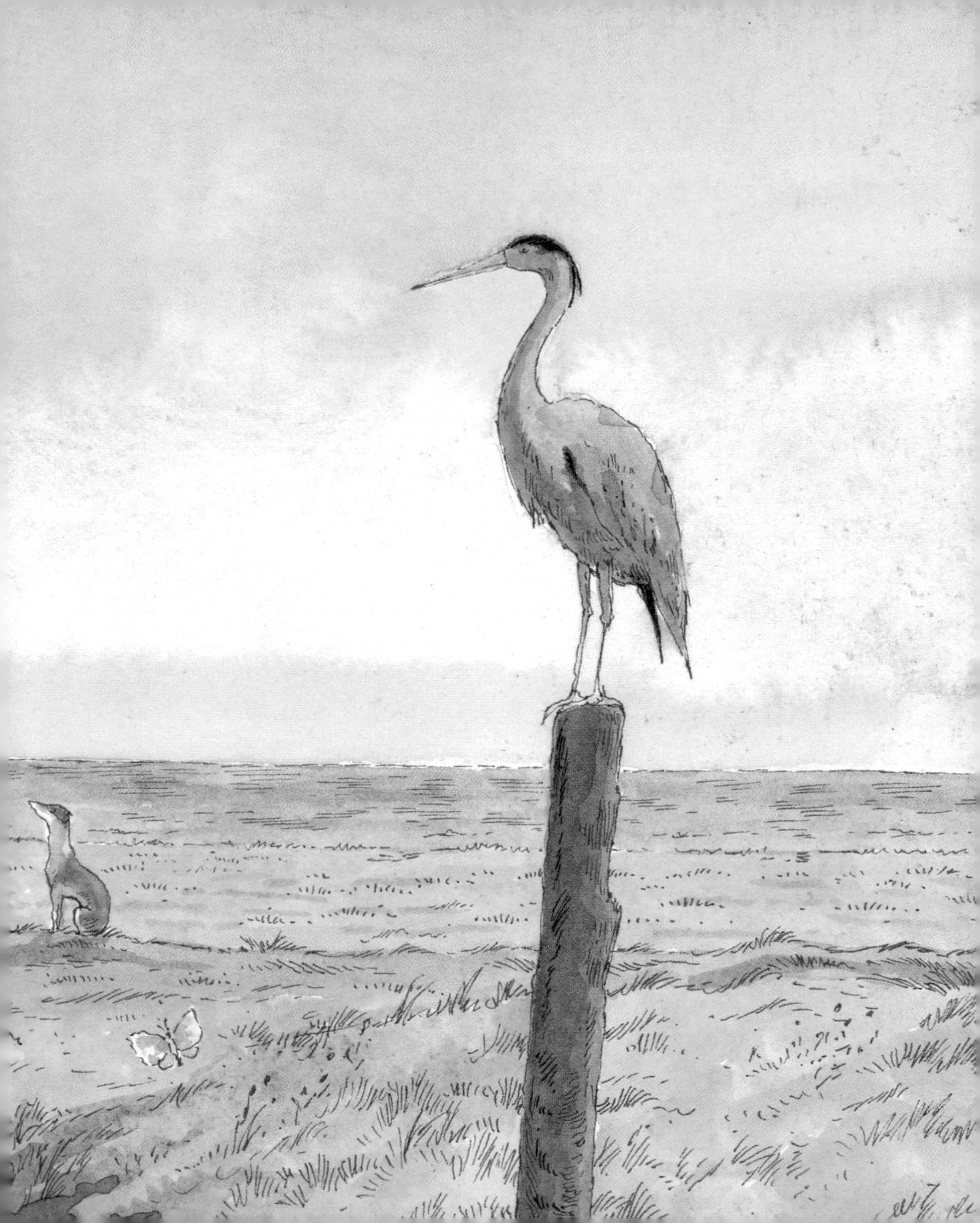

 "My home is their home too and you have no right to destroy it. Arthur called the marsh a perfect paradise. But if you build your atomic power station there, then this paradise will be destroyed for ever. You will make a hell of paradise."

Her voice gained ever greater strength as she spoke. Never before or since have I heard anyone speak with greater conviction.

"And I do mean for ever," she went on. "Do not imagine that in fifty years, or a hundred maybe, when this power station will have served its purpose, when they find a new and better way to make electricity – which I am quite sure they will – do not imagine that they will be able to knock it down and clear it away and the marsh will be once again as it is now. From my books I know that no building as poisonous with radiation as this will be will ever be knocked down. To stop the poison leaking it will, I promise you, have to be enclosed in a tomb of concrete for hundreds of years to come. This they do not want to tell you, but it is true, believe me. Do not, I beg you, let them build this power station. Let us keep this marsh as it is. Let us keep our perfect paradise."

As she sat down there was a ripple of applause which swiftly became tumultuous. And as the hall rang loud with cheering and whistling and stamping I joined in more enthusiastically than any. At that moment I felt the entire village was united in defiance behind her. But the applause ended, as – all too soon – did both the defiance and the unity.

The decision to build or not to build seemed to take for ever: more public meetings, endless campaigning for and against; but right from the start it was clear to me that those for it were always in the ascendant. Mother stood firm alongside Mrs Pettigrew, so did the colonel and Mrs Parsons; but Miss Blackwell soon changed sides, as did lots of others. The arguments became ever more bitter. People who had been perfectly friendly until now would not even speak to one another. At school Bennie led an ever growing gang who would storm about at playtime punching their fists in the air and chanting slogans. "Down with the Pettigrew weeds!" they cried. "Down with the Pettigrew

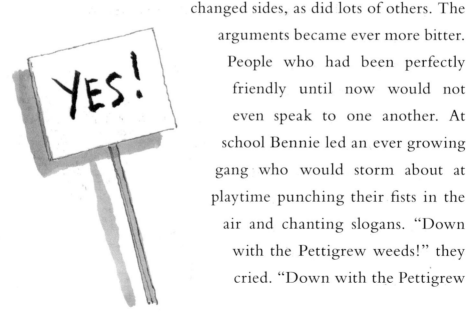

weeds!" To my shame I slunk away and avoided them all I could.

But in the face of this angry opposition Mother did not flinch and neither did Mrs Pettigrew. They sat side by side at every meeting, stood outside the village hall in the rain with their ever dwindling band of supporters, holding up their placards. SAY NO TO THE POWER STATION they read. Sometimes after school I stood there with her, but when people began to swear at us out of their car windows as they passed by, Mother said I had to stay away. I wasn't sorry. It was boring to stand there, and cold too, in spite of the warmth of the brazier.

And I was always terrified whenever Bennie saw me there, because I knew I'd be his special target in the playground the next day.

Eventually there were just the two of them left, Mother and Mrs Pettigrew. Mad Jack would join them sometimes, because he liked the company and he liked warming his hands over the brazier too. Things became even nastier towards the end. I came out of the house one morning to find red paint daubed on our front door and on our Bramley apple tree, the one I used to climb; and someone – I always thought it must have been Bennie – threw a stone through one of Mrs Pettigrew's windows in the middle of the night. Mother and Mrs Pettigrew did what they could to keep one another's spirits up but they could see the way it was going, so it must have been hard.

Then one day it was in the newspapers. The plans

for the atomic power station had been approved. Building would begin in a few months. Mother cried a lot about it at home and I expect Mrs Pettigrew did too, but whenever I saw them together they always tried to be cheerful. Even after Mrs Pettigrew received the order that her beloved marsh was being compulsorily purchased and that she would have to move out, she refused to be downhearted. We'd go over there even more often towards the end to be with her, to help her in her garden with her bees and her hens and her vegetables. She was going to keep the place just as Arthur had liked it, she said, for as long as she possibly could.

Then Donkey died. We arrived one day to find Mrs Pettigrew sitting on the steps of her carriage, Donkey lying near by. We helped her dig the grave. It took hours. When Donkey had been buried we all sat on

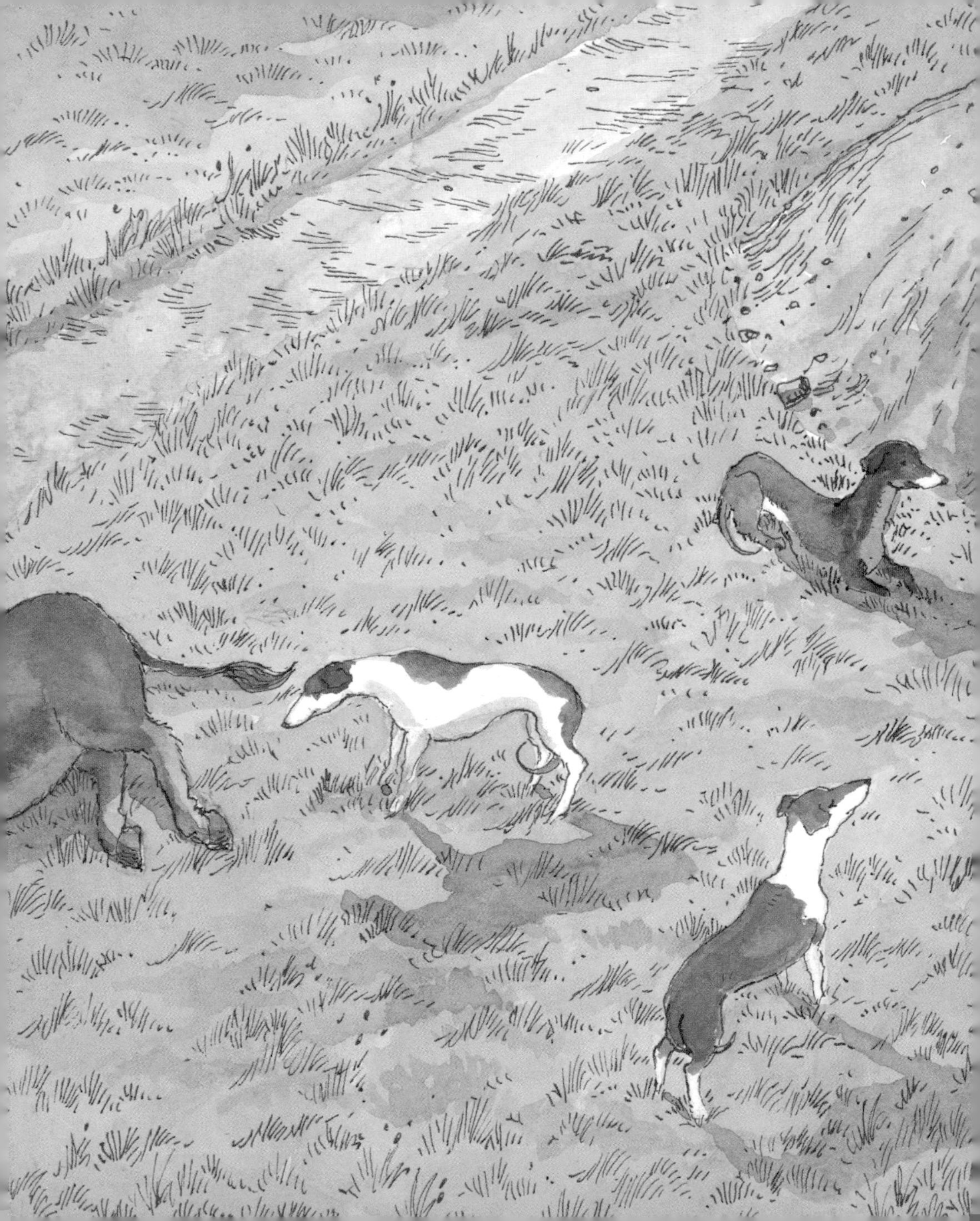

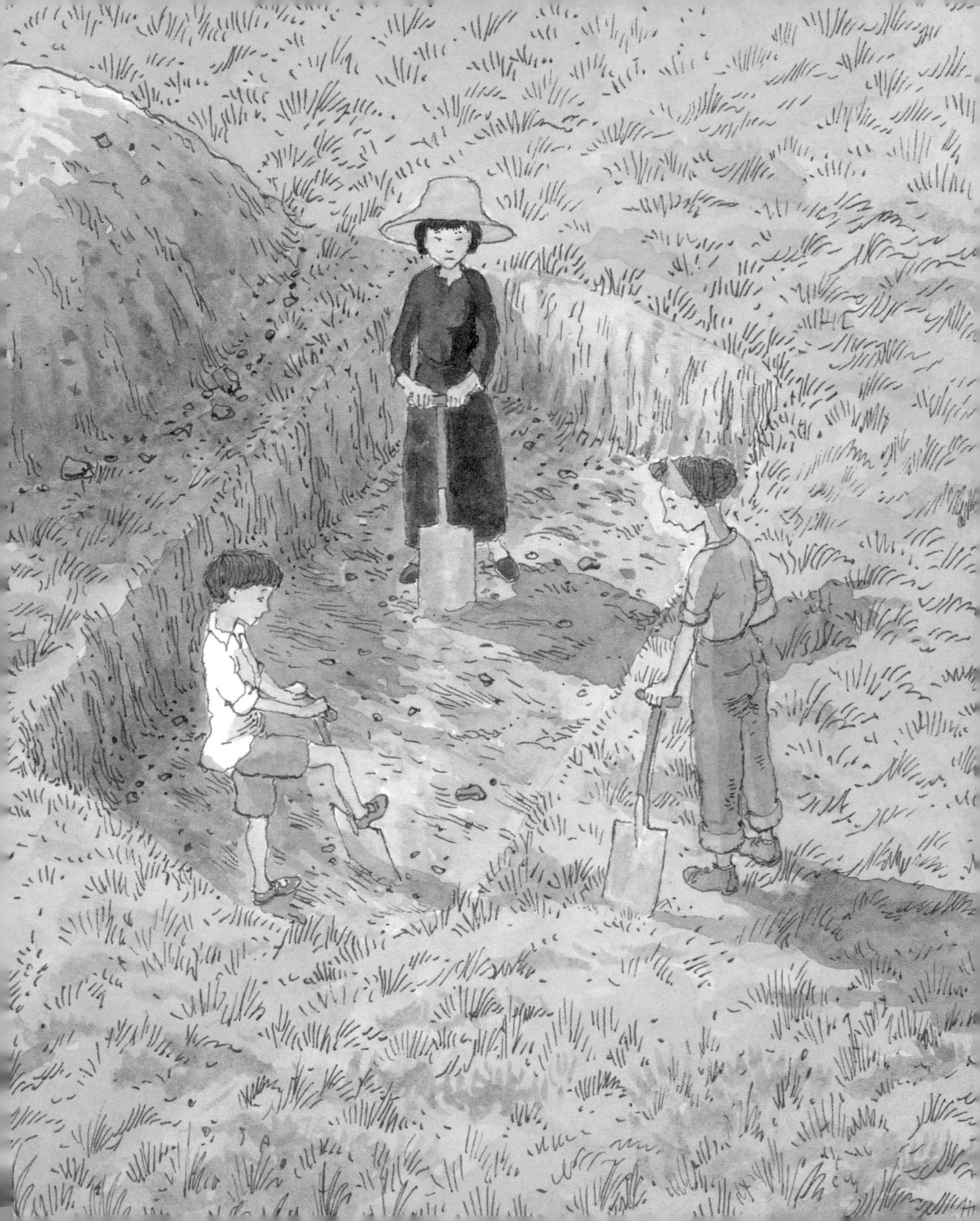

the steps in the half-dark, the dogs lying by Donkey's grave. The sea sighed behind the sea wall, perfectly reflecting our spirits. I was lost in sadness.

"There's a time to die," said Mrs Pettigrew. "Perhaps she knew it was her time." I never saw Mrs Pettigrew smile again.

I was there too on the day of the auction. Mrs Pettigrew didn't have much to sell, but a lot of people came along all the same, out of curiosity or even a sense of malicious triumph, perhaps. The carriage had been emptied of everything – I'd carried some of it out myself – so that the whole garden was strewn with all her bits and pieces. It took just a couple of hours for the auctioneer to dispose of everything: all the garden tools, all the furniture, all the crockery, the generator, the stove, the pots and pans, the hens and the hen house and the beehives. She kept only her books and her dogs, and the railway carriage too. Several buyers wanted to make a bid for it, but she refused. She stood stony-faced throughout, Mother at her side, whilst I sat watching everything from the steps of the carriage, the dogs at my feet.

Neither Mother nor I had any idea what she was

about to do. Evening was darkening around us, I remember. Just the three of us were left there. Everyone else had gone. Mother was leading Mrs Pettigrew away, a comforting arm round her, telling her again that she could stay with us in the village as long as she liked, as long as it took to find somewhere else to live. But Mrs Pettigrew didn't appear to be listening at all. Suddenly she stopped, turned and

walked away from us back towards the carriage.

"I won't be long," she said. And when the dogs tried to follow her she told them to sit where they were and stay.

She disappeared inside and I thought she was just saying goodbye to her home, but she wasn't. She came out a few moments later, shutting the door behind her and locking it.

I imagined at first it was the reflection of the last of the setting sun glowing in the windows. Then I saw the flicker of flames and realized what she had done. We stood there together and watched as the carriage caught fire, as it blazed and roared and crackled, the flames running along under the roof, leaping out of the windows, as the sparks flurried and flew. The fire engines came, but too late. The villagers came, but too late. How long we stood there I do not know, but I know that I ached with crying.

Mrs Pettigrew came and lived with us at home for a few months. She hardly spoke in all that time. In the end she left us her dogs and her books to look after and went back to Thailand to live with her sister. We had a few letters from her after that, then a long silence, then the worst possible news from her sister.

Mrs Pettigrew had died, of sadness, of a broken heart, she said.

Mother and I moved out of the village a year or so later, as the power station was being built. I remember the lorries rumbling through, and the Irish labourers who had come to build it sitting on the church wall with Mad Jack and teaching him their songs.

Mother didn't feel it was the same place any more, she told me. She didn't feel it was safe. But I knew she was escaping from sadness. We both were. I didn't mind moving, not one bit.

As I walked into the village I could see now the great grey hulk of the power station across the fields. The village was much as I remembered it, only smarter, more manicured. I made straight for my childhood home. The house looked smaller, prettier, and tidier too, the garden hedge neatly clipped; the garden itself, from what I could see from the road, looked too well groomed, not a nettle in sight. But the Bramley apple tree was still there, still leaning sideways as if it was about to fall over. I thought of

knocking on the door, of asking if I might have a look inside at my old bedroom where I'd slept as a child. But a certain timidity and a growing uneasiness that coming back had not been such a good idea prevented me from doing it. I was beginning to feel that by being there I was tampering with memories, yet now I was there I could not bring myself to leave.

I spoke to a postman emptying the postbox and enquired about some of the people I'd known. He was a good age, in his fifties, I thought, but he knew no one I asked him about. Mad Jack wasn't on his wall. Mrs Parsons' shop was still there but now sold antiques and bric-a-brac. I went to the churchyard and found the graves of the colonel and his wife with the black pencilled eyebrows, but I'd remembered her name wrong. She was Veronica, not Valerie. They had died within six months of each other. I got chatting to the man who had just finished mowing the grass in the graveyard and asked him about the atomic power station and whether people minded living alongside it.

"Course I mind," he replied. He took off his flat cap and wiped his brow with his forearm. "Whoever put that ruddy thing up should be ashamed of themselves. Never worked properly all the time it was going anyway."

"It's not going any more then?" I asked.

"Been shut down, I don't know, maybe eight or nine years," he said, waxing even more vehement. "Out of date. Clapped out. Useless. And do you know what they had to do? They had to wrap the whole place under a blanket of concrete, and it's got to stay there like that for a couple of hundred years at least so's it doesn't leak out and kill the lot of us. Madness, that's what it was, if you ask me. And when you think what it must have been like before they put it up. Miles and miles of wild marshland as far as the eye could see. All gone. Must've been wonderful. Some funny old lady lived out there in a railway carriage. Chinese lady, they say. And she had a donkey. True. I've seen photos of her and some kid sitting on a donkey outside her railway carriage. Last person to live out there, she was. Then they went and kicked her out and built that ugly great wart of a place. And for what? For a few years of electricity that's all been used up and gone. Price of progress, I suppose they'd call it. I call it a crying shame."

I bought a card in the post office and wrote a letter to Mother. I knew she'd love to hear I'd been back to Bradwell. Then I made my way past the Cricketers' Inn and the school, where I stopped to watch the children playing where I'd played; then on towards St Peter's, the old chapel by the sea wall, the favourite haunt of my youth, where Mrs Pettigrew had taken me all those years before, remote and bleak from the outside, and inside filled with quiet and peace. Some new houses had been built along the road since my time. I hurried past trying not to notice them, longing now to leave the village behind me. I felt my memories had been trampled enough.

One house name on a white-painted gate to a new bungalow caught my eye: New Clear View. I saw the joke, but didn't feel like smiling. And beyond the bungalow, there it was again, the power station, massive now because I was closer, a monstrous complex of buildings rising from the marsh, malign and immovable. It offended my eye. It hurt my heart. I looked away and walked on.

When I reached the chapel, no one was there. I had the place to myself, which was how I had always liked it. After I had been inside, I came out and sat down with my back against the sun-warmed brick and rested. The sea murmured. I remembered again my childhood thoughts, how the Romans had been here, the Saxons, the Normans, and now me. A lark rose then from the grass below the sea wall, rising, rising, singing, singing. I watched it disappear into the blue, still singing, singing for Mrs Pettigrew.

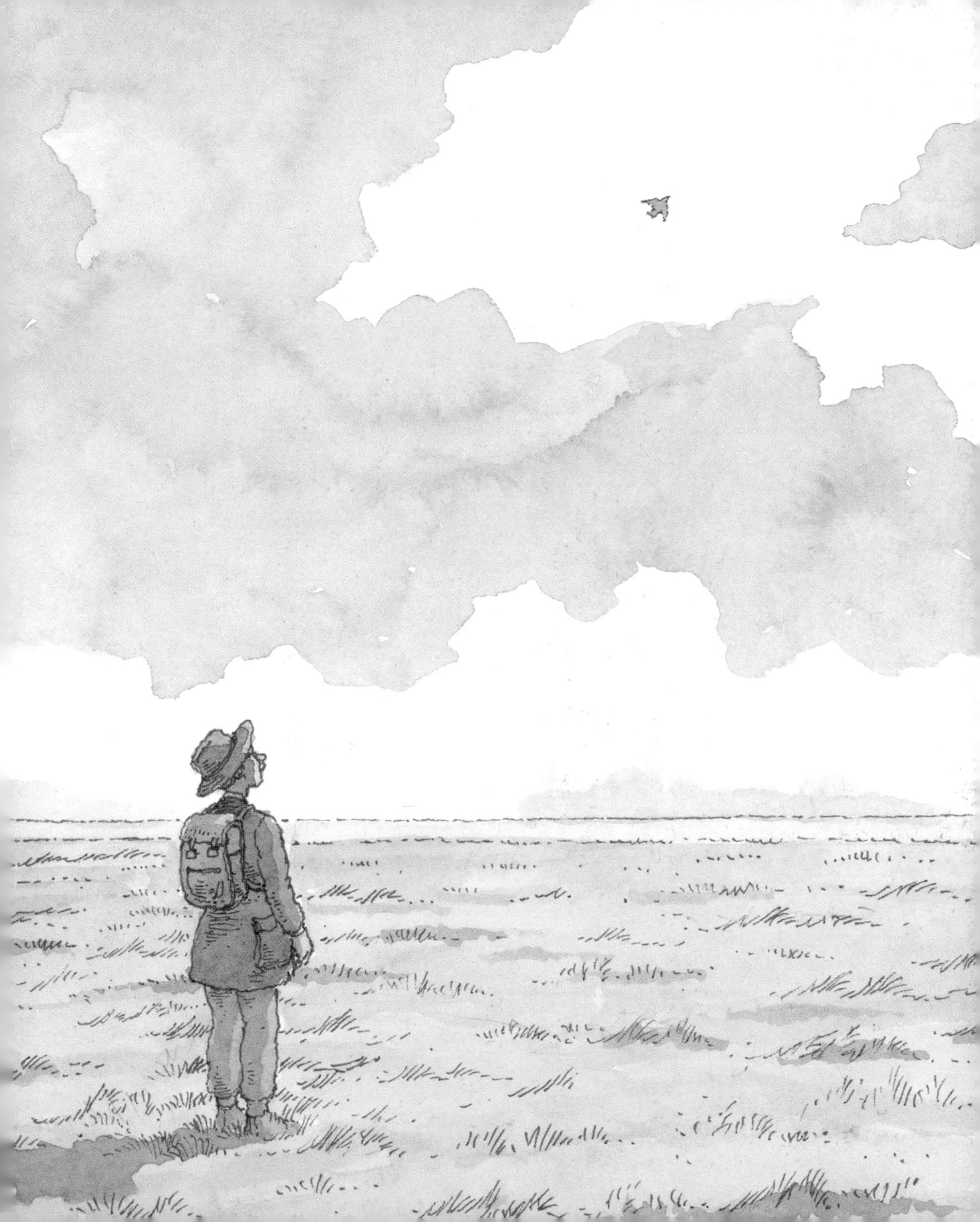

Tomas hates school, hates books and hates libraries. But the stories spun by the Unicorn Lady draw him in, making themselves part of him ... and changing the course of his life for ever.

"This book needs to be bought for every library, school and home, to share with as many children as we can, that they might experience its magic for themselves." *The Bookseller*

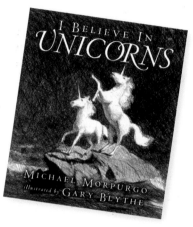

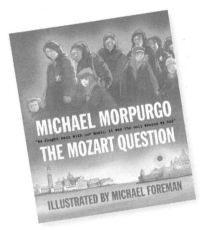

When cub reporter Lesley is sent to Venice to interview a world-renowned violinist, she discovers a long-kept secret – and learns how one group of musicians survived the full horror of war through music.

"Beautifully illustrated, this is a moving tale of secrets, lies and the past." *The Independent*

When young Michael spots a whale on the shores of the Thames, he is sure he must be dreaming. But not only is the creature real … it has a message for him.

"A thought-provoking, touching story with beautiful illustrations on every page."
Primary Times

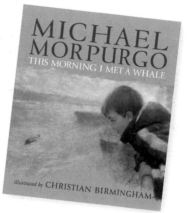

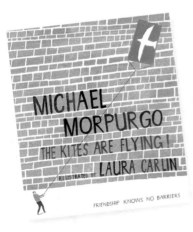

A television reporter's experiences in the West Bank reveal how children's hopes and dreams for peace can fly higher than any wall dividing communities and religions.

"Insightful and beautifully illustrated."
Daily Express

Michael Morpurgo was 2003–2005 Children's Laureate, has written over one hundred books and is the winner of numerous awards, including the Whitbread Children's Book Award, the Smarties Book Prize, the Blue Peter Award and the Red House Children's Book Award. His books are translated and read around the world and his hugely popular novel *War Horse*, already a critically acclaimed stage play, has recently been made into a film. Michael and his wife, Clare, founded the charity Farms for City Children and live in Devon.

Peter Bailey has been illustrating books for over forty years and has worked with many of today's best-known authors, including Dick King-Smith, Allan Ahlberg and Philip Pullman. Of working on *Homecoming,* he says, "I've really enjoyed illustrating this story. It's about time passing and the changes that one sees from childhood to adulthood – and about meeting, early on, someone who influences you for the rest of your life." Peter lives near Liverpool with his wife, Sian, who is also an illustrator.